CANDI

By Sujeiry Gonzalez

Corner of Press Publishing

ISBN-13: 979-8987424100

Printed in the United States of America

CHEAP SHOES VS JIMMY CHOOS

"Damn," I whisper to myself, "he looks like a snack." I press my thin, red-stained lips together, slightly biting my lower lip at the sight of him.

My chest heaves, revealing my almost non-existent cleavage. Salivating now, I watch him on tippy toes from the bar's dirty window, fogging it up like a kid anticipating Santa's arrival. Jay reaches for his drink and his muscular biceps flex involuntarily. He clinks glasses with Mary, a real estate agent at the firm we work for. His lips spread into a smile, exposing straight white teeth.

"Looks like Cognac," I say to myself as he takes a swig.

If I focus on his beverage instead of his steely blue eyes, thick black hair, and chiseled jaw, I might muster the fortitude to walk into this bar without making a fool out of myself. I shudder and flop my arms to get rid of the goosebumps that are invading my skin.

"You can do this. Just act normal."

I grab the door knob and pull, but the door won't budge. I pull again.

"What the fuck?" I grunt. I give it another yank and topple back, my right heel snaps and my clumsy ass hits the concrete.

"Shit! Shit! Shit!" I shimmy my ass from the front steps of the bar to the bodega on the right, hoping Jay didn't catch my tumbling act.

"*Tu ta bien, muchachita?*"

I look up at the hefty older man that is towering over me. He gives me his hand to pull me up from off the sidewalk. I hesitate, unsure if I should accept his offer. He's either going to shower me with *pirporos* or talk me to death about Dominican politics. I take my chances. I don't think I can get off the floor otherwise and I have to walk into this bar. I am a woman on a mission. Ever since Jay and I began flirting at work in between closings and house showings, I've longed to taste him.

"*Gracias,*" I say to the seemingly innocent Dominican gentleman.

"*No ay problem,*" he responds in a sing-song voice. "Oye, ju haf boyfren?"

Oh, no. We are not doing this, sir.

"Ahum." I clear my throat. "*Si, adentro,*" I say, pointing at the bar. "He's waiting inside."

He walks away with a shrug. I'm finally ready to make my entrance.

"Ugh, my heels," I mutter as I stare at my broken shoe. I sigh, knowing that I have two options as a New Yorker: put on the sneakers tucked inside my purse or stop by a local mom-and-pop shoe store. I peek inside my tote bag. My worn gray and pink Nike's stare back at me pitifully.

"Not today, Satan."

Luckily, in Washington Heights there are as many shoe shops as there are beauty salons. If I really want to impress Jay, I can even change my outfit. Go from business casual to Bottle Girl in 2.2 minutes.

I hobble into the first store half a block from the bar. Instantly, I am greeted by merengue and a retail associate's half smile.

"*Hola*," she says, glancing at me from top to bottom.

Her flippant expression quickly turns into a smirk as she notices my broken heel, as if she doesn't have the same pair of shoes on. I smile politely despite my desire to read her tacky ass for filth. I am not letting this lady steer me off course.

"*Los zapatos*?" I ask sweetly.

She points to the back. I follow her finger and grab a pair of red heels. They may be pleather and will surely give me blisters by the end of the night, but looking my best for Jay is worth the temporary pain.

I rush to the register, pay for the heels, and

speed walk back to the bar thanks to my Nike's. I stand by the door again and switch my footgear like I'm running the NYC Marathon.

"Be cool," I say to myself, pulling the door slowly this time.

I make my way toward him. Beads of sweat are dripping down my armpits and my hands are clammy as fuck. I take a quick whiff of my pits in case I have to dash to the bathroom to freshen up before greeting him.

"You're good," I whisper. "No, you're amazing," continuing my pep talk. "You're a freaking catch!"

Jay turns away from Agent Mary and we lock eyes. He smiles so wide I can see his dimples from a few feet away. I catch my breath in case I stumble again and break these new, cheap $30 heels. Jay waves me over. My pulse quickens. I feel a fiery blaze in my nether region. We're only inches apart now. I smile, trying my best to ignore my throbbing *cuca,* and peck him softly on the cheek.

"Hi," I say.

"Hey you," Jay says.

"Hey babe!"

I spin and come face to face with a tall, voluptuous woman. She floats over to Jay like a Disney princess. Her hair swaying behind her back as she struts over in Jimmy Choos that she did *not* just buy on 181st street. The modelesque woman beams, brushing past me as if I'm invisible. She cups Jay's chiseled jaw in her slender hands, licks her fuchsia-painted lips, and kisses the fullness of his. I get a whiff of her perfume. She smells of lilacs. She is more beautiful than I could have ever imagined.

NOT TONIGHT, ELLEN

Jay hugs her tight and turns his eyes away from me. My stomach churns. I feel like I had one too many shots of Jose Cuervo on an empty stomach and I haven't even had a sip.

"Mila," Jay says, turning her toward me, "this is my coworker, Candi."

Mila smiles sweetly, towering over me. I feel my feet swimming in the pool of sweat that's accumulated inside of my cheap heels.

"Nice to meet you," I say, extending my right hand and regretting it instantly. Because I feel like I just walked out of a steam bath and forgot to wipe myself dry. I'm sure Mila *never* sweats.

She smiles even wider but doesn't take my hand. Instead, Mila comes about an inch from my face and pulls me into a warm embrace. "Candi," she whispers in my ear, her voice as sweet and chilly as a cherry-flavored icy.

With full, fuchsia-colored lips, she plants a kiss on my cheek. Matte. Of course. Not a stain left behind. My glossy, red lipstick is probably smeared all over my mouth by now.

"Jay's never mentioned you before."

Her words almost knock me out. I'm afraid I'll fall right in front of her thanks to the shock and my personal Monsoon Season. The month of May gets me every time. And then there's the fact Jay hasn't mentioned me and her apparent amusement of it. Dig the knife in deeper, heffer! I want to shout. Only it isn't her fault. Why would he mention me? We're just coworkers with a slight flirtation. And they're...well, what are they? He's only mentioned her in passing and never said he had a girlfriend. Is she his girlfriend?

"Jay is super busy at the firm, we hardly see each other," I rush through the sentence, catching my breath while wiping lip gloss from the corners of my lips. Is there no AC up in here?

Mila nods, but I'm not convinced she believes me. The truth is that day in and day out Jay spends hours in my office. Swiveling in my chair that I willingly offer him so I can stare at his steely blue eyes. He often leans back and flexes his biceps. And in those moments, from Monday through Friday, Jay and I share stories about our upbringings, family life, and ambitions.

***

"I remember the day my mom kicked my dad out of the house for cheating," he admitted one day, "and I promised myself I'd never be that guy."

Jay rubbed his bare chin in contemplation. I wanted to say something, but I also knew it was important to give him the space to sit with his feelings and share more when he was ready. Jay is like an onion that I really want to peel - and eat. And I'm one of those rare Dominicans that hates onions.

Another first for me: crushing on a white guy. I have only dated Dominican men from Washington Heights, often meeting them locally at one of my singing gigs. As drinks flow and *merengue* blares, I flirt and pursue my Quisqueyano of choice.

"What are your dreams?" Jay changed the subject, turning his interest back to me and my story. He did that often. It made me feel seen.

"I want to sing every day of my life...even when I'm a *vieja*!" I chuckled.

"I would love to hear you sing one day," he mused, rolling his chair next to mine.

"Maybe you can come to one of my gigs," I said shyly.

Jay brought out that side of me, that timid little girl that I thought I'd outgrown thanks to music and performing on stage. Whenever I speak to him, he brings me right back and I'm at a loss for words.

"Sing something now...just for me," he teased.

Jay leaned in close. I turned my face toward him and felt his hot breath on my lips. He smelled of musky aftershave and Mentos. Like clockwork, my hands began to sweat. My *cuca* grew hot. We locked eyes for a second, my cheeks ablaze. I shut my eyes to focus on my voice. I felt like I had to give the performance of my life. Swallowing hard, I sang the chorus of my favorite song in falsetto, "Tonight! Tonight! Oh, oh, oh, oh! Tonight!"

I opened my eyes and locked eyes with Jay again. He hadn't moved an inch. Jay's lips curled up.

"Wow, you are something…" he beamed.

"So are you," I said.

"Did I hear Candi sing?!" Ellen shouted, bursting into my office without a knock on the door. Typical Ellen. She ran this real estate firm and believed she owned every corner. Her secret office nickname: Barging In Ellen.

"Yes, that was me, Ellen!" I said while quickly pushing my chair away from Jay. I wiped my sweaty hands on my camel-colored polyester pants.

"We need to do a karaoke night!" she yelped. "Now…back to work! Jay, I need you to go take a look at a new property in Rego Park."

"On it." Jay pushed off from my chair and stood up straight. Ellen turned on her heel and left in a flash with Jay behind her. And just like that, our moment was gone.

***

A drunk patron bumps me on the shoulder. I wince. The abrupt strike and pain bringing me back to Jay and Mila. Right there in front of me. The perfect couple.

"Are you ok?" Jay rests his warm palm on my shoulder and gives it a squeeze.

"Fine…fine…" My ears are burning now. I

struggle to catch my breath again from his touch.

Ok, I have to snap out of it! Mila is going to notice that I have the literal hots for her boyfriend, or whatever they are, and Jay's going to think I'm some silly schoolgirl with a crush. And I do have a crush, but I thought it was reciprocal. Yet here he is with another woman instead of taking shots with me at the bar. I really hoped that a night of drunken debauchery would have finally led to us rolling around naked in his bed. His couch. Shit, even on the floor in his foyer. Assuming his Kew Gardens condo has a foyer. We'd be so hot and heavy we wouldn't even make it to his bedroom.

"Do you want a drink?"

Jay eyes me intently, shifting his foot from one to the other as his hand rests on my shoulder. He's nervous. I've never seen him nervous. Probably because he's been caught red handed with Mila. Who, yes, is probably almost definitely his girlfriend. I mean, look at her? Large bosoms, snatched waist, and perfectly lifted and tight behind. Her long mane tickling the small of her back as she sways to a *bachata* like a gazelle. So graceful and pretty and just perfect. Straight out of a Bottle Girl catalog.

And look at me. My breasts are but a mouthful, my love handles are squeezed into my pleather skirt, and my big ass jiggles when I walk. My naturally curly hair is so voluminous that I have to pack it on top of my head like a pineapple every night before bed. And don't you dare run your fingers through it.

One tug and my curls unravel, turning my mane into a puffy, frizzy mess like a defective Transformer.

"No, I'm good."

I turn back looking for an escape. There has to be another coworker I can cling to until my best friend, Yo, gets here.

Mila leans forward and whispers something in Jay's ear, giggling as she caresses his shoulder. Her jet black hair dances on her shoulders as she cocks her head back and laughs harder, yet still so graceful. His warm grasp slips from my shoulder; I feel coolness in its place. I shiver when Mila plants a kiss on Jay's lips. She's marking her territory. I don't need to watch this show.

"Well, it was nice meeting you!"

I give them a quick wave. Jay nods, his eyes darting from Mila to me. I give him a wry smile and turn around, pushing away unfamiliar coworkers that came to party from all over the city to celebrate Ellen's new office acquisition in Cambria Heights.

"Make sure to come back and have a drink with us!" Mila calls out, her voice trailing as I walk further and further away to the back of the bar.

"Where is Yo?"

I push the bathroom door open and the door pushes back. I topple over and fall flat on my ass again, only this time I knock over someone's cocktail behind me.

"Oh, I'm so sorry, Candi!"

"I'm fine," I reply tensely, looking up at who bumrushed the door on the other side of the bathroom. Of course. It's Barging in Ellen.

"Let me get you a drink! And look, karaoke!" she shouts over 50 Cent's "P.I.M.P." pointing to a second room. Ellen bops to the music completely off beat.

"Not tonight, Ellen," I mutter.

I stand up, brush past her, and enter the bathroom. I look in the mirror. My red lipstick is creased under my lips and my feet cry in pain.

"Not tonight."

THE COMPACT NIGHTMARE

Ellen pulls my hand in an attempt to get me on stage as she croons into the mic. "More than wooooooooords," she belts offkey, "is all I ever wanted you to shooooow!"

I shake my head and mouth "no." I am in no mood to duet with Ellen. Even if Jay didn't just drop me like I have the cooties, I wouldn't get on stage with annoying, know-it-all, nosy Ellen. She yanks my arm harder and I nosedive onto her feet.

"Oh, so sorry!" Ellen shouts into the mic causing some serious feedback. She glances down at me for a moment before turning back to her adoring audience, who are only cheering her on because she signs their paychecks.

I push myself off the sticky floor and tap my nose. Doesn't hurt. I brush my finger under my nose. No blood. Ellen points to me and finishes off the song, her margarita sloshing onto the floor, "Cause I already knooooooooooow!"

I make my way to the front of the bar, hiding

behind coworkers who are too busy taking shots and interoffice flirting to notice I'm using them as a shield. My phone buzzes in my purse. I can faintly hear *La Isla Bonita,* Yo and I's favorite Madonna song.

"Finally," I murmur, grabbing my phone from my clutch to read her text.

"Candi, I have an emergency delivery. Don't hate me, hate the baby. Call you tomorrow. Love you, babe."

Great, now I have to take the NYC subway at 1am. My executive assistant salary barely covers my NYC rent and voice lessons. I refuse to pay $40 for an Uber to drive me 2 miles back to Inwood thanks to Friday night surcharges.

I swing the door open and breathe in the NYC summer air. Gas fumes, salty sweet peanuts, and ripe mangoes sold by street vendors: smells like home. Ripping my red pumps off, I sigh with relief and step into my worn kicks. I jaywalk across the street toward Fort Washington Avenue to catch the 181st A train when I hear someone call my name. I don't have to turn around to know that it's him, but I do anyway. A light summer breeze whips my curls away from my face as I watch Jay run toward me.

"Hey," he pants, catching his breath. "Why are you taking the train so late? It's not safe."

I shrug off his concern. He should have thought of my feelings when he wasn't honest with me about Mila, instead of flirting with me at work like we had a budding romance.

"It's not what you think," Jay wipes his forehead.

I take a step back because he's actually nervous.

"We're not serious. I just want you to know that."

"Well, thanks for the concern and the heads up. I hear my train coming and I really have to go."

I whip my head back around and exhale, attempting to maintain my nonchalant facade. One more minute with Jay and my mask will crumble. I'll succumb to our undeniable attraction.

"Let me take you home." Jay snatches my hand as I walk away, squeezing it ever so slightly.

I turn back. He moves in, inches away from me now. His chest heaving so closely to mine that I can hear his heart racing as swiftly and powerfully as the train rattling below me. His neck is so close to my lips, I can lick him from earlobe to clavicle. I peer into his steely blues, turn away shyly, and breathe in his musk.

"I have feelings for you," Jay whispers in my right ear, slightly licking it with his warm, wet tongue. He gives my hand an extra squeeze and caresses the inside of my palm with his thumb.

My pulse races. I face him and groan. "Me too."

I cup his chiseled jaw with my other hand. My fingertips trace his lips and I get on my tippy toes to meet my mouth with his. Jay lowers his head. I want him to swallow me whole. Only he pulls back.

"Let's go then," Jay responds coolly, dropping my hand and stepping back. He stands a whole foot away from me now. With his chin, he points to his parked Mercedes, turns around, and walks ahead of me. I shake my head, confused by his sudden coldness.

"I don't understand," I murmur into the midnight summer air.

Jay slows down, twists his head, and calls, "Candi?"

I unstick my feet from the concrete and shuffle over to Jay who waits in front of his car. When I reach him, I search for an answer behind his hesitant eyes. He holds my imploring gaze for only a second before opening the backdoor of his car.

"What are you? My Uber?" I chuckle, hoping to bring some levity to the moment. Hoping he'll snap out of whatever this is so we can go back to who we were just minutes ago.

"Candi, come in!" Her rich, sultry voice calls from inside.

I suck in some air and say, "Hi Mila!" before taking the backseat behind her. Jay drops his head and closes my door. I stare out the window, holding back tears, as the engine purrs.

Mila twists her neck to face me. "Why would you take a train this late, silly?"

I'm not sure if she's teasing me out of concern or teasing me because she knows she's won.

"I do it all the time," I mumble, shutting my eyes so she can just stop talking to me.

"Well, it's not safe," she states firmly before turning back around.

"Where do you live, Candi?" Jay asks.

I open my eyes and look up at his rearview

mirror. His piercing blue eyes plead with me. For what? To not blow up his spot with Mila? I roll my eyes and he flinches.

"Broadway. 212th street."

Glaring out the window, I focus on the world outside of this compact nightmare. I lazer in on the homeboys on the corner, the 24-hour bodegas, and the 5-story buildings that house thousands of immigrant families. The club kids that tumble out of local lounges and bars. The 21-year-olds that spill tonight's dinner on the curb after one too many shots and later call a booty buddy or an ex to take them away from that very moment. I focus on anything but here. Because here is where heartbreak lives. Here is where Mila cups her hand inside of Jay's minutes after he held mine.

FORBIDDEN FISH IN THE SEA

"Aaaaaaah!" I groan, kicking the covers off my feet.

"Ow! Candi! Watch it, babe!"

Eyes squinted, I poke my head from under the pillow like a crab in a shell. "Sorry. I forgot you were here."

Yo yawns and stretches her long, mahogany legs. "You don't remember that you called me last night crying like you lost a puppy? Only you don't have a dog."

I wince and rub my temples, recalling the five Fireball shots I gulped at home after last night's embarrassment. Getting all cute for an incredible night of drinks and a potential hookup with Jay only to meet Mila. Mila holding Jay's hand during the 40-block ride to my apartment. Jay and I on the street corner milliseconds away from kissing before he turned into...turned into...who, exactly?

"Ugh!"

I flip over on my tummy and regret it instantly,

my stomach churning and throat burning. I hide my head under my pillow again, pressing down hard enough to block the morning sun.

"Babe, it's okay. There are other fish in the sea."

Yo rolls over like the catch-of-the-day and throws my pillow off my head and to the floor.

"But I have to see *this* fish at work."

Side by side, she peers into my dark brown eyes intensely, holding my gaze without blinking. It's a thing she does to make me laugh and to pull me out of my woe-is-me-why-am-I-never-chosen funk. Believe it or not, this unrequited thing is a pattern of mine, and Yo has always been there to mend my longing heart. I've lost count of the times she's yanked me from my small, NYC closet after being rejected for a singing gig or ghosted by a guy. Surrounded by shoe boxes, I sit there, crying in frustration. Because I know that at 30 years old it's becoming much harder to meet the man of my dreams and to keep my dream of being a professional singer alive.

I burst out laughing when Yo makes a funny face, her eyes bulging out of their sockets.

"Just get another job," Yo giggles.

"What?!?"

"It's just a job to pay the bills, right? You're focused on your singing career, so why does it matter?"

I love how much Yo believes in me and my talent, even when I'm losing hope. I won't admit it to her though. She won't let me give up even when I know that, logically, it's what I should do.

"Cause...rent." I flip over and stare at the ceiling. "This job has potential, Yo. I can get my real estate license. Make real money so I can stop...surviving."

"Don't worry about money, babe. I can help you. You know I always have your back."

A successful OBGYN with her own practice at only 30 years old, Yo has bailed me out time and again. She's the only person I can count on. As much as Mami believes in my artistry, she's too busy galavanting with whatever new rich guy she's hooked. And I've never even met my dad.

I turn to Yo and frown. "I can't let you save me again."

I know she means well, but I'm tired of feeling like a charity case. It's beginning to feel as embarrassing as riding in the backseat of Jay's Mercedes like a toddler.

"Candi, you're my best friend. And I have the money..."

"Here you go with your savior complex." I chuckle before jumping on Yo to lighten the mood and change the subject. I don't want to talk about my pathetic life anymore.

Yo laughs as I tickle her ribs. "I did single handedly deliver twins last night *and* save the mom's life, like when Lebron saved the Cavaliers from losing to the Warriors thanks to his insane block," she says in between giggles.

I groan. "Please! Not a basketball reference."

"You better suck it up. Joel is coming over soon

for brunch and we're talking basketball. It's our thing."

I roll my eyes. Watching basketball is as dreadful as hearing Ellen sing karaoke.

"Shit!" I turn on my stomach again and reach for my phone on the floor. "I have to email my boss."

"Knock! Knock!" a voice calls from outside my bedroom door. "You all decent?" Joel swings the door open.

"Hellooooooooo!" I yelp. "I didn't say you can come in, Joel. And how did you get in anyway?"

"I left him my key underneath the door mat," Yo responds, waving her brother in.

I shoot up from the bed and cover my chest with my pillow, shooting daggers at Joel with my eyes. He has a tendency to barge in due to 22 years of imposed friendship.

Joel is Yo's twin brother, a bonus friend by proxy. We grew up in the same building as kids. Their mom worked the night shift at a jewelry factory three times a week and dropped Yo and Joel off at my apartment, where Mami babysat neighborhood kids to make ends meet. Yo and I became best friends over playing dress up and choreographing Madonna songs. Joel, on the other hand, irritated me to no end. Even as adults, he teases me like when we were kids. He doesn't take anything but his corporate marketing job seriously, including romantic relationships. Let's just say Joel has a new flavor every month. Unfortunately, Yo and I have the dishonor to entertain them because Joel invites them to every club, bar, and dinner party. Typical guy shit, he can't be alone for a second.

"It's nothing I haven't seen before," he chuckles, sauntering into my bedroom.

Furious, I chuck my pillow over to Joel who catches it with one hand before sitting at the foot of my bed, his eyes roaming from my eyes to my lips to my tits.

Not bad, Candi Cane." Joel raises his eyebrows and licks his lips, they're as pink and lush as freshly cut strawberries.

"Joel," Yo shouts at her twin. "Stop hitting on Candi. She is *not* like your other girls."

Joel looks at Yo and shrugs, she could always put him in his place. According to Yo, being born first, even if just by 4 minutes, makes her the eldest twin - and the boss.

"So, we're doing brunch or what?" Joel asks, watching my ass with his peripheral vision as I stand to stretch.

"I'll buy some bagels and bacon, per usual. Candi, start making the mimosas." Yo shoots up from the bed, throws on some black and white Adidas, and walks toward the bedroom door. She spins on her heel.

"Samesies?" she adds. Joel and I both nod.

Yo slams the door shut leaving Joel and I alone. I make my way across my tiny bedroom to the bathroom, brushing Joel's back as I walk by. The hairs on my arms stand at attention. I furrow my brows. Why do I feel a knot in my stomach? Is it anxiety or...butterflies? I scurry to the bathroom to escape this sudden longing for Joel.

He's like an annoying brother to me albeit a sexy one. He's always been hot. Since adolescence, he's gotten attention from girls. And for a split second at 16 years old, when Joel, Yo, and I crashed the senior prom, we almost kissed. Joel and I jokingly slow danced to K-Ci and Jojo's "All My Life" while Yo ran to the bathroom to spike our Coke with the rum she snatched from their father's liquor cabinet.

"All my life!" I sang happily, cocking my head back while using my diaphragm.

"Sing, Candi Cane, sing!" Joel cheered me on as he pulled me in closer and wrapped his hands around my waist.

"I've dreamt of somcone like you!"

With my index finger, I pointed at Joel and smiled widely. He beamed and tightened his grip, our groins pressed against each other.

"Oh yea?" Joel crooned, his full lips inches from mine.

"Maybe," I whispered, our lips grazing.

"Watch out! Watch out! I got drinks!"

Yo pushed through the crowd with three cups in hand, pushing away slow dancing couples with her hips. Joel dropped his hands from my waist and I took a few steps back.

"Hey!" I yelled, waving Yo over to us.

"Here you go." Yo handed Joel and I our cups, filled to the brim.

"How are we supposed to dance now?" Joel

teased, sneaking me a look.

"We finish our drinks fast, brother!"

Yo grabbed my hand with one hand and Joel with the other and pulled us in like a sandwich.

"One, two, three!" she hooted. On three, we chugged, chugged, chugged and danced the night away.

***

That's exactly it, I think as I swing the bathroom door open. I can't do this to Yo after 20 years of friendship. I turn ever so slightly and catch Joel's bedroom eyes gazing at me seductively. We hold our gaze for what feels like hours before I shut the door.

My chest heaves, feeling as if it's going to explode. I press my back against the door. I close my eyes and picture Joel. His jet black, clean-cut hair. The sunlight beaming from the window and brightening his coffee-colored eyes. The dimples on his cheeks that deepen when he smiles wide. His mocha skin glowing. His luscious, juicy lips inches away from mine that night at senior prom now seducing me right in my bedroom.

I moan, bringing my hand underneath my white, satin pajama top. I cup my small breasts. I flick my nipples. They're already at attention thanks to Joel undressing me with his eyes. My fingers trace my areola before I stick them in my mouth and wet them with my warm tongue. Fingers wet, I find my nipple again. I feel a burst of warmth coming from my pussy and hurriedly bring my fingers to her. I moan again, louder now, unable to contain myself. Throbbing now, I insert two wet fingers deep inside, thrusting as I imagine Joel inside of me. Oh, how I long to feel him. To taste him.

I gasp, almost there, almost at climax. My breath quickens, my fingers move faster. My thumb caresses my clitoris in perfect circular motions.

"Oooh," I cry, "Oh God, oh God, oh God!"

Release. I open my eyes and exhale, feeling a mix of ecstasy, sweet relief, and confusion.

"Shower," I whisper.

I walk into the tub and turn the knob. Water runs down my face, reminding me to put on my shower cap to protect my recently washed curls. I look around but can't find it.

"Yo," I say. She showered last night and left it in my bedroom. I wrap myself with my red robe, swing the door open, and come face to face with Joel.

"You need any help?"

I gulp. "How long have you been standing against the door?"

"Long enough," he says softly.

Joel leans in, inches from my chest. The heat permeates from his body and warms my insides all over again.

The door jiggles. "Hello! Why is this locked?"

"Yo," I whisper. "Wait...why did you lock the door?" I say hurriedly, hoping to get an answer before she kicks it down.

Joel stands back and clears his throat, avoiding eye contact and my question.

"Coming!" He smirks, winks at me, and unlocks the door.

Yo pops her head in. "Bagels!"

I manage to smile and follow Joel out of my bedroom and into the kitchen. Yo is leading the way, as she always does. Joel trails behind her and I behind him. He places his right hand behind his back, palm up. My heart skips a beat as I place my hand in his and he caresses it with his fingertips.

IF HE COULD SEE ME NOW

"You ready?"

Yo shouts from my living room as I squeeze my thick thighs and ass inside my fuschia dress. Those damn bagels we ate earlier were too good to resist. And this is why I'm stuffing myself - and not sliding into - this new outfit.

"Almost!" I pant, wiping my brow and smoothing over the dress with my hands. I pick up a matte coral lipstick and cover my thin lips.

"You won't budge this time," I say to myself in the mirror, turning my head side to side, inspecting for any smudges.

I take a step back to admire my outfit. The heart-shaped neckline and underwire setting prop up my small chest, giving me a little extra cleavage. I turn and smile as I admire my round, high-set ass and *curvitas*. One of the many blessings of being Dominican.

"If Jay could see me now," I murmur, flipping my curly hair and posing. Especially since I feel so much more confident after my earlier...umm...interaction with Joel.

I don't even know what to call it. We haven't spoken since he left my apartment after our usual Saturday BBM (Bagel, Bacon, and Mimosas). And I can't talk to Yo about it. I tell her *everything.* But what would I say about this? That I masturbated in the bathroom while thinking about her twin brother? That he turned me on *so* much with just one glance that I had to get off at 11am? That he heard everything and loved it?

I shudder. "Shake it off, Candi." I crack my neck, roll my shoulders, and exhale.

"Candi, we have to go!" Yo calls again.

I walk out of the bedroom door, smile, and grab my best friend's hand. She could never know. Joel and I will never be a thing. I love her too damn much.

***

Yo and I push our way to the bar and wave down the bartender. I glance around the room for fresh meat, also known as hot, single guys that I haven't yet dated or rejected. Being a single girl in NYC is becoming increasingly difficult, particularly if you attend the same events, bars, and lounges. I just can't stay away from Washington Heights.

"Is Pedro coming?" I ask Yo.

She nods, still focused on grabbing the bartender's attention. He winks and saunters over.

"Two Proseccos, please." Yo flashes her dazzling

smile, exposing straight, bright teeth. "What's your name, babe?"

"Carlos." He winks at Yo, puffing his chest and throwing a towel over his shoulder.

Yo flashes her engagement ring with a wiggle of her fingers and pushes me front and center. "This is Candi."

I give Carlos, the newest Vivere bartender, a little wave and poke Yo in the ribs.

"Candi, huh?" he says, "so, you're sweet?"

Carlos flashes a smile. I try to not respond with a snarky, "how original," but he's too busy to notice my irritation. He hands us our drinks. I bring the flute to my lips and take a sip.

"Well?" Yo says.

"I think I've had enough bartenders. Especially bartenders that work *here.*"

The thought of dating another man who takes shots for a living forms a knot in my stomach. Yo rolls her eyes and faces me.

"It's just fun, babe. And with everything that happened with Jay last night you might need to release some tension. You need an orgasm - Doctor's orders!"

If she only knew that I orgasmed hours earlier while thinking of Joel. And that he listened from the other side of the door.

"*Ven,*" I grab Yo's elbow. "Let's circle the room."

"That's the spirit!" She laughs.

We wander the club, making our way through crowds of patrons celebrating birthdays, bachelorette parties, and a Saturday in the city. It's packed with lots of prospects, yet no one catches my eye. Yo tries to help, pointing at a potential here and there. I shake my head every time.

"Maybe I should go." I sigh, twisting my neck toward the door. "I'll stay with you until Pedro gets here."

"He's coming soon. His shift should be over, he's had a rough night in the ER."

Yo grabs her iPhone from her Gucci clutch and scrolls through Pedro's messages with knitted eyebrows.

"Do you want me to stay?" I place my hand on her shoulder, knowing the pressure she feels to be Pedro's everything, especially in times of stress.

Pedro is an amazing guy. I love their relationship and how they met. They were part of a mutual doctor friend's wedding party. After one too many drinks at the reception, Pedro, who's timid and reserved, made a beeline to Yo to make his move. Only he stumbled over his words and spilled a glass of Scotch all over her white Dolce dress. (She says the dress was cream, but it was in fact white. Yo wears what she wants when she wants - even when it upsets a bride.) Yo was annoyed with this mishap, refusing to give Pedro a real shot after the wedding. But he persisted and won her over when he bought her a brand new white (not cream) Dolce dress.

Then there's the side of Pedro that tightens up like a ball of yarn when stressed and irritated. He gets in these funks often, shutting down emotionally and locking himself up in his bedroom to brood for hours a day. Communicative by nature, Yo finds it difficult to maneuver this part of Pedro's personality. She tries to give him space, but explodes after weeks of physical and emotional withdrawal. Still, she loves him, and Yo is persistent and committed. She doesn't give up on anything or anyone easily.

"No, you can go, babe." Yo gives me a half-smile and rubs my back. "Ah, look! There's my guy!"

Pedro shuffles over to us and goes straight to Yo, wrapping her in an embrace.

"I'll leave you two to it," I say, patting Pedro's back as he nuzzles his face inside Yo's neck.

I spin on my heels and sigh, hoping that one day I'll find an unconditional love like theirs.

WET RIDE

Despite the humidity sticking to my caramel skin, I decide to take a walk down Haven Avenue. Other than Yo and Joel I don't have anyone else to paint the town fuchsia with. Yo has her hands full with Pedro, and I don't know how I'll face Joel ever again. I can't stop thinking about how my tummy fluttered when he caressed my hand. And the look of satisfaction on his smug face, silently acknowledging that he hooked me after all of these years.

"No," I say to myself, making my way down Cabrini Avenue. "Joel is Yo's brother. Her twin. I cannot cross that line."

I gaze up at the sky, the stars twinkling brightly despite the thick, polluted city air. They shine in spite of it. I shake my head and chuckle. What am I, a philosopher now? And where am I going anyway? I look ahead and notice a new bar. Born and raised in Washington Heights, I know my 'hood like the back of my hand. A new bar may pop up every minute, but I stay in the know of every opening and every bartender's name. What can I say? I like winding down with a glass of something. And I do have a weakness for bartenders.

"*Did* have a weakness for bartenders," I remind myself as I swing the door open and enter The Hive. Maybe the owner is a fan of bees - or Queen Bey.

I zoom toward the bar only to realize there is no one inside.

"How new is this place?" I mumble.

I whip out my phone to search for reviews on my DominiHeights Facebook group when I hear someone call out, "Come on in!"

The bartender appears from the back and waves me over.

"Um, I think I'm going to go." I begin walking backwards, keeping my eyes on him in case he's a serial killer, when I trip and fall *again.*

"Ow!" I wince as a shooting pain hits my ankle. I blink quickly, trying to gather my bearings. Did the bartender throw some black magic my way so he could lock me in the basement?

"Candi?"

Ok, I think I'm going insane because that voice sounds just like...

"Jay." I gasp.

He's in front of me now, squatting on the floor and inspecting my right ankle. I grimace as he presses gently.

"It's not broken," he hypothesizes, "or you would have kicked me." Jay smiles at me, his steely blues twinkling like the stars I admired minutes ago.

"Come on."

He grabs my waist. I wrap my arms around his

neck as he lifts me off the ground. I nestle my face into his shoulder and melt into him.

"Let me take you home so you can put some ice on it." The huskiness in Jay's voice sends shivers down my spine.

"You need anything, boss?" the bartender calls.

Boss? Jay owns The Hive? I look up at him from the comfort of his shoulder.

"Just close up." Jay calls.

The bartender nods. Jay tightens his grip on my waist as he swings the door open with his foot and walks us outside.

The NYC humidity greets me again. As Jay stomps down the street toward his Mercedes, beads of sweat collect underneath my arms and breasts. I look up at him and wonder if he feels the heat, but his forehead is perfectly dry. His neck, only inches from my mouth, smells of musk and lavender. I long to nibble. Cover him with wet kisses. I inhale and close my eyes as I bob and weave in his arms, as if I live on a cloud amongst the stars.

"We're here," Jay looks down and whispers.

He opens his car door with one hand while still holding me tightly. Jay lays me down in the passenger seat.

"Let's rest your foot on the dashboard," he says with my foot in his hand. Only my dress is too tight.

"Let me..." I whisper, scooting up my dress.

Jay's eyes scan my thick legs, come up to my thighs, and linger on my lacy red thong that's now slightly exposed. He glances up at me, locking eyes, and leans in. His lips graze mine as his large hand pulls the seat belt over my chest slowly. *Click.*

He slides his hand across my belly and then under my belly button, close enough to my pussy to cause her to throb. Jay looks at me with bedroom eyes, holding my gaze for what feels like forever. He licks his lips. His hand moves south slowly. I arch my back and open my legs wide, giving him permission to enter. He presses his lips against mine just as his fingers pull my thong to the side. I open my mouth and his wet, warm tongue greets me. It dances with mine as his fingers massage my nub and enter me one by one. I gasp, arch my back, and move to his rhythm as his digits penetrate me deeper. He sucks my lower lip. He ravages my neck and licks me from earlobe to clavicle, his fingers going deeper and deeper, faster and faster.

"You're so wet," Jay groans.

"I'm going to cum, oh, Jay, I'm going to cum!" I squeal.

My body tenses. His thumb rubs my clitoris quicker now. His fingers pump and pump and pump.

"Ooooooooo, aaaaaaaaaa, aaaaaaaaaa, aaaaaaaaaaaaa!" I scream, pulling his hair as he bites my neck. My body tenses. My toes curl.

"Aaaaaaaaaa, aaaaaaaaaaaaaaaaaa, aaaaaaaaaaaaaay, yes! Aaaaaaaaaaaaaaaaaaaaaa!"

My pussy gushes. I collapse into the seat, covered in sweat and tingling all over.

Jay pulls his fingers from my pussy and smirks. "Well, that happened."

I smile shyly, too exhausted and exhilarated to question what this means. To wonder amongst the moon and the stars about this serendipitous encounter. At this moment, all I can muster is, "It sure did."

OOPS!

My eyes flicker open. "That dream was too real," I groan, flipping over from my stomach to my back.

"Ow! Shit!"

I prop myself up on my elbows and look at my ankle. Wrapped and swollen.

"Oh my God...it was real?"

I drop down on my bed again, reach for my iPhone, and begin to scroll through text messages, hoping to see a text from Jay after our fun in his car. It's all coming back to me now, the night's details often do after a good night's rest. Jay drove me home and, despite my insistence that I finish *him* off, he assured me it was best that I rest my foot. But that didn't stop me from sending him a naughty text message in the middle of the night.

"Spam, Mami, Ellen, Ellen, ugh, why is she texting me on a weekend?" I say to myself. "Yo, Yo, Yo, Yo...ok, I have to call Yo." I make a mental note. "Joel...Joel?"

I pause, hesitating to swipe up to read his words. What if he wants to talk about what happened? I shake my head, "It's Joel! He probably just text a silly meme."

"Candi Cane, you free?" it reads.

I drop my phone.

"No, no, no, no, no..." I rub my eyes, hoping to wake up from this nightmare. This thing with Joel cannot be a thing. I pick up my phone again and exhale.

"Hey, what's up?"

Speech bubbles. Stop. Speech bubbles. Stop.

"Just say it!" I yell at the phone.

"Meet me at Vivere for Sunday brunch?"

I sigh, my fingers hovering over the keyboard as I decide what to do with my best friend's brother.

"Sure. 11am." I type and hit send.

"11am it is," he responds.

I pull the covers over my head, wondering why Jay hasn't responded and how to get out of this mess without ruining the best relationship I've ever had... my friendship with Yo.

***

I fluff up my curls in the mirror, swing my apartment door open, and almost twist my other ankle when I almost smack into Joel.

"What are you doing here?" I ask nervously. "You said 11am at Vivere."

Joel looks down at my ankle, smiles at me sheepishly, and points to the wheelchair behind him. "I figured you'd need a little help."

I snort. "Well, I do not need a wheelchair, thankyouverymuch!"

"What are you going to do, hobble there like a

vieja? You're going to hurt yourself."

Joel looks at me concerned. He points at the chair again, a stern look on his face. "Sit down."

"Fine." I turn around and prop myself on the chair. He rolls me down the hallway toward the elevator.

"Wait," I turn around and look up at him. "How did you know I sprained my ankle?"

"You don't remember?" he stops dead in his tracks as I scan my brain.

What did I do last night? Why did I drink three Fireball shots at home before going to Vivere with Yo? And what does my night with Jay have to do with Joel? I can't remember, but I have to think to save myself from embarrassment.

"Oh, yea, I remember now. We're good. Keep rolling."

I point toward the elevator and Joel laughs behind me.

"Ok, good. I'm glad you remember what you said last night."

"Me too," I mumble.

***

"Hey Maria, a table with enough space for *una invalida,*" Joel snickers while motioning to me.

"Girl, what happened?" the hostess, Maria, says while glancing at my foot. "You look like you had a rough night." She smirks and stares at Joel.

"Just a fall, Maria," I clear my throat. She's as gossipy as self righteous churchgoers that live for scandal.

"Right this way you two."

We follow her lead and are seated at a large table.

"Does Yo want her usual?" Maria asks.

"Yo's not coming," Joel states. "Just bring us our usual. Thanks, Maria."

Maria nods, looking at Joel with a half smile. "I wondered when you two would get together."

"We're not..." I mumble as Joel takes my hand.

"Thanks, Maria," he responds with a smile.

I look back at Joel and scan my memory. I remember everything that happened with Yo at Vivere last night. The new bartender bringing us Proseccos. Pedro showing up distressed. Going to The Hive, spraining my ankle, and...well, how can I forget what happened with Jay in his passenger seat? Why can't I remember what happened with Joel? Did that new bartender slip me a mickey? Am I losing my memory at 30? Do I need to lay off the Fireball?

"Excuse me. I have to use the ladies room." I snatch my hand back and push back my wheelchair.

"I can take you," Joel begins to stand from his seat.

"No, it's okay, I got it." I roll away quickly.

"See, I can roll right on over," I shout, Joel getting further and further away as I make a beeline from the bathroom to Vivere's courtyard.

I park under a fake palm tree and scroll through my phone to read our last text exchange. My fingers stop.

"I want you."

I gasp, covering my open mouth with my hand and realizing my grave mistake. That message was meant for Jay.

"Oh my God, oh my God, oh my God," I whisper under my breath, rolling back and forth in my wheelchair.

"*Mira! Ten cuidao!*" a patron yells after I almost snip her toes off.

I mouth a "sorry" and return to my text message. My heart sits in my throat. I have no idea how to fix this. How to break the news to Joel that although we've always had chemistry and a flirtatious friendship, we could never be a thing. My friendship with Yo is too important and she would flip. She's so overprotective of Joel and, yes, even me.

Yo is the momma bear of our clan. We prance around her like baby cubs waiting for her direction and support. What would happen to our tribe if Joel and I were intimate and became an actual thing? Or worse, if our love affair grew hot and heavy, full speed ahead, only to be snuffed out in three months or less. This is my pattern. At 30 years old, my longest relationship has been a mere 6 months, and the last 3 months were off and on. Mostly because I refused to let it go, begging for my ex's attention and validation. God, I was such a fool.

My brain runs a mile a minute to conduct an exit strategy. I cannot go back to the table. I cannot have a conversation with Joel about my accidental text. I need time to think. To find a way to get out of this

mess thanks to two orgasms that have rendered me
delirious.

QUICK GETAWAY

"My stomach is killing me," I shout as I wheel over to Joel. "I really have to go…you know…"

I look back at my rear and grimace, hoping my lie will keep Joel as far away from me as possible. At least for the time being.

"Oh, no…can I get you anything?" Joel rises from the table and begins to approach me.

I wave him off. "No, no, I just really need to get home. Too much partying last night."

"That'll get you every time," Joel chuckles, stuffing his hands in his pockets and shuffling his feet. He looks a little bit heartbroken. I don't want to cause him any pain.

"I'll call you, okay?" I rush through the sentence. "So we can talk."

Joel's face comes to life again. He smiles wide, exposing his dimples. I fight the urge to hobble over to him, embrace him, and put my fingers inside his dimples like I did when we were teenagers.

***

"Let me see how far it can go," I said as I stuck my

fingers in each cheek, pushing them further inside.

"Ouch, you're hurting me!" Joel shouted, giggling in spite of the pain.

"It's just so...different. It's kind of cute, friend." I inspected his cheeks with my hands, turning his face from side to side.

"Thanks...*friend*," he repeated, agitation in his voice.

My hands dropped from his face and I smacked his chest playfully. "Stop, Joel! Just...stop."

He shrugged sheepishly before muttering, "I tried."

***

"Are you sure you're okay?" Joel asks, snapping me back to the present moment.

I shake off the pang of guilt that I feel off of my face, unknitting my furrowed brows. Joel has always cared for me romantically. He has always wanted to be more than friends. Even now, as I leave him alone at Vivere with his unspoken desires and feelings, he's still taking care of me. But I can't. How could I? How could we? I don't want to have to choose between Yo and Joel. I don't want to have to choose between Joel and Jay.

"I'm fine, I promise." I nod, hoping this will provide him with some reassurance that it's not him, it's actually really me who messed up here.

"I'm going to go now, but stay for brunch, okay? Don't let me ruin your day."

Joel puffs his chest and exhales slowly. A way

to calm his nerves and ease the tension. He nods, strolls over to the bar, and greets our favorite bartender, Ramon. I manage to wheel myself outside without breaking any more hearts or toes.

EPIPHANY

"He hasn't called or text and I haven't seen him at work," I tell Yo, who resurfaced from Pedro's clutches three days after our short night at Vivere.

According to Yo, Pedro is in a much better place, but something tells me she needed to escape. In our Pedro countdown, he still has 48 hours to revert back to his laid back, easy-breezy self.

"When was the last time you text him after you orgasmed in his car?" Yo asks matter-a-factly.

"Damn, Yo, not even a smile? Are you judging me?" I feel judged.

"That's what happened, Candi. And no, not judging. It's sexy as fuck even if he has a thing called a girlfriend."

"They're not a thing. He kind of told me so outside the train station." I don't know if I'm defending him or myself, but it doesn't feel good either way.

Yo shrugs. She knows I have to learn the hard way. When I set my sights on a man and he makes me feel the way Jay does, all tingly and filled with passion, I can't let go until I've tried *everything*. It's that same passion, resilience, and diligence that allows me to bounce back whenever I don't book a singing gig.

"I text him goodnight last night and then again this morning asking if he wanted to grab a coffee before work tomorrow," I redirect the conversation, looking down at my phone in my hands. I stare at our message thread.

"Well, you'll see him tomorrow, right?" Yo reminds me.

"He's scheduled to come in, but what do I say to him?" I bite my lower lip, recalling all the men that I've pushed too hard and every relationship that I've continued to pursue even when the guy I'm chasing wants to cut ties.

To be fair, my exes were never honest about wanting to end our relationship. They would simply grow distant and detached, text less, and, eventually, stop making plans all together. The gradual ghosting.

"Candi, please don't bend over backwards for him or any other dude, okay?" Yo pleads with me, softening her position.

"How's your foot by the way?" she asks.

"It's fine. Just a little tender, but I can walk on it."

She cups it in her hand and presses. "Any pain at all?"

"Nope, I'm good, Yo. Promise."

She stops inspecting my foot, stands over me, and leans in for an embrace. Her warm, long mahogany arms wrap around me and I relax instantly. Cradled in her arms, I look up and peck her on the cheek.

"Thank you, best friend. I will try to value myself more."

My voice cracks and I burst into tears. Not just because of Jay's avoidance or my fear that he's going to discard me, but also because I'm keeping a huge secret from Yo. That I, Candi, Yo's best friend and soul sister, have a thing for her twin brother.

SAD PUPPY

"Candi! I neeeeeeeeed you!"

Ellen calls from the back office seconds after I burst through the door, huffing and puffing due to hobbling 20 blocks from the E train. Thank you, stalled subway car!

"Coming, Ellen!"

I run into my office, swing the door open, and fling my purse on top of my desk. I miss my mark and it falls on the floor. The contents inside my tote bag spill over.

Exasperated, I groan, trying to shake off this awful weekend and week, and so far, morning. Jay still hasn't responded to my texts. Not a peep from him after my coffee invite for today. To top it off, I have to start my day with Ellen.

"Yes, Ellen, you called?" My tone changes from an around-the-way-girl that wants to rip your head off to Employee of the Month.

"I need you to meet Jay on the Austin St property," she grabs a stack of papers from her desk. "He needs these closing papers pronto, Candi. It's a cash offer!" Ellen yelps with excitement. Nothing makes her happier than over-asking price cash offers.

"Not a problem," I lean in and take the folder from her hand, plastering a smile.

"Now, Candi! Now!" Ellen shouts before shutting her office door.

I sigh, run to my office and quickly pick up my belongings from the floor. The last thing I want to do right now is work with Jay, but this is what I get for shitting where I eat.

I wave goodbye to my coworkers as I swing the door open. Hobbling to the corner, I hail a yellow cab. Tires screech as the cab driver does a U-turn and pulls up. I slide into the leather seat.

"2031 Austin Street, please."

The cab driver hits the gas. We fly down Metropolitan Avenue. I close my eyes and try to relax.

"Bing!" I rummage through my purse, searching for my cell phone and find it underneath a crumpled napkin. It clings to my golden encrusted phone case. Pulling on it carefully so it doesn't rip, the scribbled block letters appear.

"Candi Cane, sing your song," I whisper, reading back the note. The memory of that night rushes in.

***

A year ago, Joel accompanied me to a talent showcase on Bowery Street after Yo was called in to Columbia Presbyterian to deliver a baby. It was my first time singing to a bunch of *gringos* since I mostly book gigs in Washington Heights/Inwood. Usually at Vivere or at another locale where everyone knows my name. The comfort of familiar faces loosens me up and I belt song after song with the band jamming in the background. But that night was different. From the A&R reps in the front row to the artists handing out demos and professional photographs with attached CVs, I felt like a small fish in a big pond...and I'm not a strong swimmer.

"Shake that shit off," Joel comforted me. Our eyes locked as he leaned in, resting his forehead on mine. "You are the most talented woman I know."

I squirmed, uncomfortable with his praise and our closeness. My skin grew hot and I really had to pee. The latter a nervous tick that appears right before every nerve racking performance.

"I don't know what to sing anymore. I don't think this is the place for my favorite Miriam Hernandez song."

I leaned back, attempting to create some physical distance between Joel and I. Only Joel pulled me in closer, wrapping his strong hands around my waist. I didn't know whether it was my nerves or his unwavering belief in me and my talent, but I felt myself melting, just like I did when we almost kissed at our non-senior prom. A wave of heat washed over me. I wanted to devour him. To pull him close, wrap my legs around him, and dance a bachata with this tongue.

Joel cocked his head, his lips close enough to taste. He brushed a wild curl away from my face, smiled, and purred, "Candi Cane, sing your song," right as he planted a kiss on my cheek.

And I did sing. Actually, I saaaaaaaaang. I may have not gotten a record deal out of that performance, but I will never forget Joel scribbling those words on a napkin that night. As I took the stage, he sat in the front row, swaying to my voice, holding up this very napkin as encouragement.

***

"Miss, we're here!" The taxi cab driver barks from the front seat, breaking me out of my reverie. I stuff the napkin and my phone inside my purse again and begin searching for my wallet.

"This should cover it." I hear Jay call.

He hands the driver a $20, walks to the back seat, and opens the door for me. With one hand in his pocket, he reaches for my hand with the other. I take it and step out of the car. His eyes scan my peach-painted lips before landing on my eyes.

"Nice to see you, Candi."

A smile slowly spreads across his face.

"You...you..." I stammer before cleaning my throat, "too."

Jay places his hand on the curve of my spine. I shiver although it's 90 degrees outside.

"I got the papers that you need."

I clutch the folder in my hand as we walk inside the commercial space that Jay is selling. He turns to face me and nods, dropping his hand from my waist as a young couple approaches.

"Larry. Beatrice. We're ready," Jay states, his deep, raspy voice commanding the space and penetrating my very core.

I hold my breath and begin counting from 0-20 to calm the fuck down. Another technique that I use to calm my nerves when I am on stage. Only I'm at a commercial real estate closing for my job! What is wrong with me? What hold does Jay have on me that I can't be at work without shaking in my fake red bottoms? I feel like an idiot.

I shift in my heels and turn my head toward the door, plotting my escape to save myself from further embarrassment.

"Candi."

Jay turns his back from Larry and Beatrice and faces me, his brows furrowed.

I blink. What did I miss?

"The papers." He points to the folder in my hand and frowns.

"Oh, yes, yes."

I rush over to Jay and almost trip on a crack on the floor. He grabs me by the elbow just in time. Relieved and embarrassed, I smile sheepishly. Annoyed, Jay rolls his eyes at me and turns back to the couple with a smile.

"Candi here is quite a klutz," Jay quips.

I nod feverishly, trying to save face although my heart hurts a little. He's right, I am a mess. I spill everything, I'm always late. And I keep a yearlong memento stuffed inside my purse.

"Shall we?"

Jay motions to Larry and Beatrice to sit at a table. They walk away without a second glance. Jay chuckles while engaging in more small talk, ignoring me as I limp out the door like a neglected puppy.

COLD CHICKEN

"All set, Candi?"

Ellen pokes her head inside my office. She sniffs, her nose searching for my lunch.

"Ooh, what are you eating?"

Without an invitation, Ellen runs to me at my desk and picks up a piece of chicken from my plate. I glare at her, nostrils flaring. But she barely notices. She's too busy devouring my *chicharron de pollo* and chewing with her mouth open.

"You know, Candi, I went to the DR once."

Ellen towers over me and takes one more bite.

"The people, the beaches, the culture," she says while chewing noisily, "simply beautiful."

A tiny spitball from her mouth lands on my arm. I flinch and fight the urge to push her off my desk and tell her to lay off my lunch. I do not need her intrusive, rude, bossy energy after how Jay's treated me. He finger banged me, ignored my texts, and called me his klutzy, uncoordinated coworker. Is that how he sees me?

Ellen leans in, her long, bony index finger hovering over my plate. Underneath my breath, I growl like a rabid puppy that's been beaten down and starved.

"Ellen, I need your signature. Papers are on your desk." Jay interrupts, sauntering in and grabbing Ellen's attention away from my plate before I bite her finger off.

"Oh, sure, sure. Thanks for the snack, Candi!" Ellen sing-songs. She rushes out, eager to sign on the dotted line.

Jay closes the door once Ellen leaves. I gulp, trying to stay strong as he glides over to me because he's been treating me like a slut he picked up at a bar. I bite my lip, fighting the urge to demand answers. Remembering my promise to Yo: don't chase. Value myself.

He pulls up the chair in front of me, takes a seat, and leans in. "Candi…" he murmurs, his eyes lowered. "What are you doing this weekend?"

"I…don't know," I lie.

I actually have a singing audition this weekend, but I'm afraid that if I say so he won't say what I hope he's going to say next.

"Good. Let's go away then."

He reclines, folds his hands, and rests them over his crotch. I bite my lip again as I trace the outline of his bulge with my eyes.

"And where do you propose we go?" I ask cockily, trying to sound indifferent.

"The Hamptons, of course."

Jay shoots up from the chair, cusps my face, and traces my lips with his thumb.

"I have a house with a pool…it'll be fun."

His deep, raspy voice reverberates under my skin. I tremble under his gaze and touch, inhaling his musky scent. I shut my eyes. I breathe him in deeply and feel his hand drop from my chin.

"I'll call you," he whispers into my ear.

I hear the door slam shut and finally open my eyes. Jay's gone back to work like the Golden Boy he is while I sit here with a plate of cold chicken and a wet pussy.

BABY, QUÉ MÁS?

"Baby, ¿qué más? Hace rato que no sé na' de ti!"

I belt out KarolG's "Provenza," swaying my hips from left to right. Music lifts me higher than any orgasm or cocktail. It transcends my pain and heals every heartbreak. I walk over to my radio, reach for the knob, and blast the volume.

"Taba con alguien, pero ya estoy free."

I spin in my living room and hug myself tightly, imagining Jay as my dance partner. He might be a white boy from Long Island, but he has some rhythm. We've danced a song or two at company parties. Grinding to reggaetón like a couple in love.

"Love? Is this love?" I ask myself, shaking my head. "Don't get ahead of yourself, Candi."

I plop myself on the couch and stretch my legs on my ottoman, tilting my head back to sip my Prosecco. I grab my phone and begin scrolling on Amazon for a new bikini. And maybe a new dress altogether. And a nightie with a garter belt? I only have two days to plan my wardrobe for my weekend in the Hamptons with Jay. Thank goodness for Prime.

Bang! Bang! Bang! I jump out of my seat,

Prosecco splashing all over my pink work blouse.

"Shit!"

I charge toward the door, ready to give my neighbor a mouthful. Whether I'm singing till the cows come home or listening to my favorite bachata, she lives to complain about the noise. Not today. It's only 6pm. I am well beyond my rights to listen to music in my apartment at full blast before 9pm! Scowling, I swing the door open, ready to give her a mouthful.

"Why haven't you hit me up? It's been three days since you left me at brunch."

Joel stands in front of me, his arms stretched from one end of the door to the other. My eyes pop out of their sockets. I stand there speechless.

"*Papi, nos perdemo', nos parqueamo' y lo prendemo*," KarolG sings in the background.

"Well?" Joel glares at me. I've never seen him this upset.

"I've been busy...with work," I spit out, unsure of what else to say.

"Too busy to talk to me? About your text?"

Joel drops one hand from the door and rubs his face. Exasperated, he begins to pace.

"I'm sorry," I whisper. I really am. I got us into this mess and now...now...

"Now what? Huh?"

I step back, taken aback by our...telepathy? How did he...? I close my eyes and exhale deeply. Focus, Candi. Mitigate this fucked up situation. Get yourself out of it *fast.*

"Joel," I whisper, my eyes still shut.

I feel him closer. His hard pecs press against my chest. He slides his fingers around my waist, low enough to touch the crack of my ass. My breath quickens.

"Candi Cane," he whispers in my ear. "I want you too."

Joel nibbles my earlobe and rubs the tip of his nose on my cheek. Planting soft kisses on my lips. Naturally, I lift my arms and wrap them around his neck. Eyes still shut, I tilt my head and get on my tippy toes to reach his mouth. Joel gently sucks my lower lip. Then my top. My lips part and our tongues move together in perfect harmony as "Provenza" plays on a loop in the background.

"*Pa' la seca algo bebemo', y cuando nos emborrachemo.*"

Joel cups my ass and lifts me up off the ground. I yelp in excitement as he carries me inside, slamming the door shut with his foot. He buries his head in my chest, licking in between my cleavage.

"Oh Candi," he moans.

Joel lays me on the couch, pressing his body on top of mine as we continue to kiss. I can feel his manhood and cup it. Stroke it. His coffee-colored eyes deepen. His mouth opening wider with every stroke. Joel reaches for my hands and lifts them above my head. Unbuttoning my blouse with his teeth, it falls to my sides. I'm braless and he smiles, licking his lips as he brings his mouth to my breast. He flicks my nipples with his tongue, gently licking and sucking.

"I moan. "That's the spot."

"Oh, I haven't hit that yet."

His mouth crawls from my right nipple down to my belly button, kissing along the trail. He gets to my sweet spot. His strong hands run down my arms to my breast and caress them as his soft, wet tongue finds my clitoris. I gasp as it flutters over her, warming her up with every twist and turn, before he penetrates me with his tongue. My back arches. Joel brings his tongue back to my throbbing clitoris. He inserts his digits, pumping them in and out, in and out. I grind to his rhythm.

"Wait..wait," I squeal. "I want you inside of me!"

Joel kisses my inner thighs before coming up for air and pressing his chest against mine. He strokes my face and kisses me gently.

"You ready for this?" he asks, smugly.

"Are you?" I muse.

"Well see, won't me?" Joel says with a smile.

I nod, giving him permission to keep going. He kisses me deeply before thrusting his pelvis and entering me. He grips my ass, lifting it up from the coach, as he penetrates slowly, over and over again. I caress his broad back, tracing every muscle with my nails. I swerve underneath him. He drives his dick deeper and deeper.

"That feels so good," I groan.

"Candi Cane..." Joel breathes heavily, burying his head in my neck.

My pussy pulsates, getting closer and closer to

orgasm. He thrusts faster. I pump my pelvis along to his rhythm. Joel comes up for air, locking eyes with me and pressing his forehead against mine. We move in unison, to the rhythm of "Provenza."

"Sing to me, Candi," Joel groans.

I begin to sing in between squeals and heavy breathing, *"Una de reggaetón ponemo* ...aaah...aaaah...I'm cuming."

On cue, Joel pumps deeper, faster.

"Keep singing, baby." He grunts, his face wincing with pleasure.

"A donde nos podamos...aaaah....aaaah...aaaaaaay.....querer."

My toes curl. I keep singing. *"Nos podamos...*oh my God...oh my God...*nos podamos...a...comer."*

My body tightens. Joel, his eyes still on mine, speeds up his movements.

"Joel...Joel...aaaaaaaah!" I whimper in delight as he moans loudly, bursting from inside out.

We go limp in each other's arms. Joel presses his lips to mine and our tongues find each other again. I giggle, exhausted and ecstatic all at once. He smiles, sucking on my lower lip before letting go. He tilts his head back, gazes into my eyes, and whispers, *"Baby, ¿qué más?"*

THE MORNING AFTER

I yawn and stretch out my arms, poking my ass in the process. It's the morning after and Joel is sleeping beside me.

"Hey there, you're going to get him excited," Joel rumbles from slumber, pointing at his penis with his chin. I giggle, snuggling up against him. He kisses my neck from behind, pulling me in closer to his big spoon.

"Hmmm..." I groan. "This is..."

"What you've been running from for years." Joel chuckles, stating his version of events as fact.

"I was going to say nice, but you had to get all cocky."

I yank the pillow from underneath my head and slam him with it playfully.

"Oh, yea, you want a pillow fight? You know I'll win."

Joel jumps to the other end of the bed and grabs my body pillow, ready to attack.

"Bro, not everything is a competition," I scoff,

eyeing the three pillows on the loveseat beside me.

Joel follows my eyes. We lunge for the pillows simultaneously. I grab them first and we laugh, pulling them from each other like a game of tug-of-war before toppling onto the bed.

"You are a mess!" I laugh, catching my breath.

"You are breathtaking."

Joel rolls on top of me and kisses my lips in between my chuckles.

"Joel?!"

My hands stop rubbing Joel's back and shoot straight above my head. We've been caught red handed.

"Candi."

There is tension in her voice. A slow, burning intensity that will erupt any minute now, like a tea kettle that's been left on for too long. I hold my breath as I lay there, hands limp over my head. Joel lays on top of me, frozen. I rack my brain, trying to find the words to explain to my best friend of 20 years why her twin brother is straddling me right now.

"How long has this been going on?" Yo shouts.

I can feel the steam rising from within her. I stare at Joel. My eyes pleading with him to get off of me. To say something to her. Joel kisses me on the lips gently. Yo gasps at his audacity. My eyes bulge and I frown. I want to shout at him, what the fuck, Joel? Why are you rubbing this in? He pushes himself up and sits beside my limp body, finally facing his Yo. I can't move. This is the worst thing I have ever done. This is the worst way she could have found out about us.

"Sis, it's okay," Joel finally speaks. "Candi and I -"

"Oh!" Yo scoffs. "Candi and I? So this *has* been a thing. And it's been happening behind my back."

She is screeching now. I'm afraid she might trash my place, just like she destroyed her ex-boyfriends car when she caught him cheating with a mutual friend from college. Yo keyed his car, popped his tires, and broke his windows. And she did it without a drop of alcohol. She's that scary when she allows herself to abandon control.

"Calm down, sis, this just happened."

Joel motions to me as I lay stiffly in bed, like a corpse that's about to be embalmed.

"Candi," Joel calls me softly.

He knows there are two things that I'm terrified of: never making it as an artist and ruining my friendship with Yo.

I heave, coming to." We shouldn't have done this, Yo, I'm so sorry!" I shout in between sobs.

I finally sit up and face my best friend and her disappointment, fury, and pain. She squints, like she's seeing me for the first time. Her jaw clenches. She makes a fist. Snot rolls down my nose and down my quivering lips, covering my entire mouth. I don't care to wipe. I deserve this, to be dirty and snotty and covered in shame. Joel wipes a tear from my cheek. I smack his hand away. He clenches his jaw just like Yo. He's a replica of his sister.

"I..." I gasp, trying to find the words to fix this.

"I love..." I feel light headed.

"I love you, Yo!"

Yo snorts, cocking her head back and reveling in my despair. "The only person you give a shit about is yourself, *babe*."

She sneers at me, spins on her heels, and storms out. My head drops, curls toppling over and blocking my vision. Yo is right. She has always taken care of me, helping me pay my rent and supporting all of my dreams. She's even beaten up some of my loser ex boyfriends. And I repay her by sleeping with the person she loves the most. Because I can't control my impulses. Because I am a selfish, careless, terrible person.

"I'll fix this, okay?" Joel whispers, cradling me in his arms.

I go limp and sob inside his embrace.

WORLDS COLLIDE

It's been 48 hours since I've spoken to Yo. It's the longest we've lasted sans communication. Or the longest I've let her ignore me.

When studying for the United States Medical Licensing Examination, Yo placed my calls on Do Not Disturb. I showed up to her apartment building anyway carrying two speakers over my head and Bad Bunny's *Dakiti* on cue - her favorite reggaetón song. It didn't take long for Yo to run out of her first floor apartment to join me for an outdoor dance party. With her long legs exposed, thanks to her booty shorts, and her hair wrapped in a dubi, she released her stress and shook her ass right beside me. We twerked in the middle of 212th and Seaman Avenue, ignoring the Caucasian onlookers. They scowled with outrage at these two Dominicans making a scene assuming we're uneducated hoodrats when I have a Bachelor's of Arts in Theater and Yo is a child genius. She graduated from high school at 16.

Once the song finished, Yo back ran to her apartment to continue her studies, like the disciplined student she has always been. But not before wrapping her lmbs around me and entangling me in an embrace.

***

"Candi!" Ellen shouts from her office. "The files!"

Her voice brings me back to reality. I grab a stack of paperwork to hand to Ellen. Only 5 minutes before I clock out and clock in to my weekend with Jay. He's picking me up at my place tomorrow at 9am. Just thinking about where this weekend in the Hamptons will take our relationship sends chills down my spine.

As for Joel and I, that's over. Despite his incessant texts during the last 48 hours stating the contrary. Jay and I can be the real deal without the drama. He hasn't mentioned Mila at all. At least not in passing at the office. Besides, if she was a factor, he wouldn't be taking me away to his house on Long Island.

Two minutes to 5. I jog down to Ellen's office, folder in hand. On Fridays, I purposefully wait until the last minute to meet her deadlines so she doesn't assign me another task.

"Here you go, have a great weekend!"

I practically throw the paperwork at her desk. I spin on my heels, tote bag in hand, and race toward the door. The August heat hits my cheeks. I smile, taking it all in because despite Yo refusing to answer my calls, texts, and musical pleas (I played *Dakiti* last night outside her window and she did not acknowledge me), I am thinking positively. I am manifesting an amazing life with Jay, where my best friend, Yo, is my Maid of Honor and the only bridesmaid at our wedding.

"Candi!"

Joel runs up in front of me, out of breath. He wipes his brows before reaching for my hand. I take a giant step back, taking my hand with me.

"What are you doing here?" I ask.

"We haven't talked since..."

His voice trails and I know that I've hurt him. Joel De Santos is actually affected by a woman.

"But Yo," I sigh.

As much as the idea of Joel excites me, this can't happen. Yo's silence speaks volumes.

"She will get over it once she realizes this is *real*."

Joel takes a step toward me again. I breathe in his woodsy scent mixed with the humid NYC air. He tilts his head, cupping my chin and bringing my lips towards his.

"We can't," I whisper, moving my face away.

His hand drops and jaw tightens. I feel a warm hand resting on the curve of my back.

"Everything okay, Candi?" Jay asks smugly, standing next to me.

I nod and press my lips, unsure of how to respond at this moment. Joel recoils and stuffs his hands in his pockets. I can see the outline of his fists as they sit inside the seams. I can see the pain in his eyes.

"I'm Jay." Jay extends his hand toward Joel, his head cocked to the side.

Joel shakes his head in disapproval and chuckles.

"The infamous Jay!"

My cheeks burn. I watch him rub his chin mischievously. Yo and Joel share the same vindictive streak. What are you going to say, Joel? Don't make this worse than it has to be?

"Infamous." Jay smirks, scanning my body with his blue eyes. They rest on my ass for what feels like forever before turning to Joel. He squints, his head still cocked, before sputtering, "What's your name again?"

"Joel." He seethes.

Jay furrows his brows and looks up at the sky, pretending to search his thoughts. "Doesn't ring a bell. Guess that doesn't make you infamous, huh."

Joel's nostrils flare. He buries his fists inside his pockets. Deeper and deeper, the seams at their breaking point. He looks just like Yo when she's about to blow. I hold in my breath, bracing myself for him to swing, spew, or pop off. Only he doesn't. Joel throws his hands up in front of him and nods.

"That is true, my man. That. Is. True."

He bows his head, turns around, and walks away without a second glance.

"Are you ready for tomorrow?" Jay asks, squeezing my waist and pulling me closer to him.

"Ready." I whisper.

Although at this moment, I'm not quite sure.

MAYO-R SURPRISE

I come face to face with the largest house I've ever seen. Four stories, majestic columns, perfectly trimmed, bright green shrubbery, a front lawn as expansive as my entire block: it's straight out of "Selling Sunset." I look up at Jay, intimidated by his status and wealth. He unlocks the door and swings it open.

"Wow!" I gasp, surveying the foyer.

The white marble floors sparkle, waxed to perfection. I can see my reflection. The winding staircase leading to an even more expansive landing.

"8 bedrooms," Jay brags.

He walks ahead. I follow him into the kitchen quietly. I stand in the corner, watching Jay as he grabs food from the refrigerator and places them on the counter.

"Make me a sandwich."

He waves over the items before strolling into the living room and plopping himself on the couch. My brows furrow. Is that a command? I bite my lip, making my way toward the kitchen island. I stare at the jar of mayo, two slices of whole wheat bread, a tomato, a pack of American cheese, and one plate. Jay didn't set out a plate for me. I grip the tomato and breathe, trying to settle myself and clear my head. I've felt confused since Joel and Jay met face to face.

"It's just a plate, he just forgot," I mumble to myself.

"Candi, grab me a beer!" Jay calls from the sofa.

Every bone in my body wants to shout, "Get it yourself!" But this is what I want, right? To be with Jay. Commanding, untouchable, complicated Jay.

"Coming!" I sing back.

I finish making his sandwich quickly, snatch a can of Coors Light from the refrigerator, and place his plate and drink on the coffee table. Jay pats the seat next to him on the sofa. I stand over him, look down at my feet, and wring my hands. Jay takes a bite of his sandwich, oblivious to my discomfort, which began on the car ride over. He picked me up outside of my apartment building and immediately commented on my 'hood.

"God, how can you live here?" He said in disgust, as if I live in a rat's nest.

"It's home. This is where I grew up," I said, defending my neighborhood.

"You'll see what a *real* home looks like soon. Come on, get in."

Jay set my carry-on inside his trunk, walked over to the driver's door, and put on his seatbelt. Embarrassed all of a sudden, I slid into the passenger side. As we drove past rows of buildings, bodegas, and beauty salons, the colorful streets coming alive with *mi gente* as they got ready to begin their Saturday mornings, I wondered if I made the right choice. I looked over at him, unsure of what was next and what to expect.

"We'll be there in 3 hours," he said.

I nodded, shifting in my seat. Jay looked over at me and smiled, his softness coming through despite the tension that I felt between us. Maybe it's just me.

"I'm excited," I whispered, hoping to snap myself out of this confusion.

"Good," he replied, his eyes back on the road.

Now, here I am. Bringing him a sandwich and feeling uncomfortable as fuck. Like I'm standing in front of a stranger. I look over at the door. Should I escape this mess or give Jay a chance to prove that he didn't bring me out to the Hamptons to be his maid? Maybe he's just tired? It was a long drive from the city.

I smile weakly and sit down next to him, my hands clasped on my lap like a good school girl. I clear my throat. Jay takes another bite.

"So, what do you want to do today?"

"I figured we'd...you know..." he responds with a mouthful of food.

I wait a beat until he swallows so he can keep his bits of food to himself.

"We'd what?"

Jay puts his sandwich down on the plate and wipes his hands and mouth with his napkin. He faces me. He rests his warm, large hand on my knee, sliding it up my inner thigh, inches away from my pussy. I frown and scoot back on the couch. Jay tightes his hand on my thigh.

"You're hurting me!" I yell.

"Where are you going?"

His eyes intensify as he inches forward and leans over me. I fall onto the sofa, the coolness of the leather fabric chilling my shoulders. He tugs at my thong. I shut my legs and clench my pussy.

With his fingers still lodged, he snorts, "Are you serious?"

I can smell the mayo on his breath.

"I don't want this." My voice breaks.

"This is *all* you've wanted."

Jay shoots up and glares at me from his end of the sofa. I scoot my skirt down and slide further away from him. I don't know who he is, who he's become? Then again, have I ever truly known him?

"You can get out," Jay retorts coolly.

He takes another sip of beer and grabs the remote control, blasting a baseball game at full volume. Flustered, I think about what to say next. I don't want to upset him any further. I don't want to stay here, but I have nowhere else to go.

"You're still standing here?" He seethes.

Another swig of beer before he slides his phone from his back pocket. Jay presses a button and coos, "Hey you."

He laughs and waves me away. I hold back tears as I charge for the entrance. I grab my suitcase from the foyer, slamming the door shut. Outside now, I face Jay's majestic home, admiring its beauty despite the ugliness that lives inside.

STRANDED

"Yo, please pick up!" I whimper into the phone, pacing in front of Jay's mansion. "Jay tried, he...I'm stranded in the Hamptons...I don't have enough money for an Uber...I *need* you."

I throw my cell in my purse and bend over. "Breathe," I wheeze.

I stand up straight. Sun in my eyes, I squint to find a place to sit and rest my feet. Serves me right for trying to impress Jay by wearing these cheap, red pumps again. For coming all the way out here without a backup plan. For believing in Jay when he showed me who he was - a douchebag after one thing - that night in his car.

"No, this isn't your fault." I give myself a pep talk. Or is it? I walk toward a water fountain, pausing mid-step in contemplation: am I to blame for my messy life?

As the water spouts from the top of the bird structure, I realize that Jay always played these games. He knew I would attend the company party, yet he brought Mila despite our heavy office flirtation. Jay wanted to rub her beauty and sophistication in my face. To make me jealous. And when I felt defeated, he reeled me back in by telling me he liked me while Mila sat a few feet away, tucked away in his parked car.

He's always been a sleazeball, so why didn't I see it? I look at the bright, blue sky, hoping to find answers in its vastness. Eyes closed, the sun's rays heat my face. I remember our intimate moment in his car and him ghosting me soon after.

"That was all me," I sigh. "He showed me who he is, but I kept pushing like a *pendeja*."

I kick off my pumps. My bare feet touch the concrete floor. "Because you always want what you can't have."

That's the game that I play. A dangerous game of Validate Me, where I chase the unattainable guy that treats me like shit as a way to prove my worth to myself. A game that I'm tired of playing because I always lose, left with swollen feet, a bruised ego, and a shattered heart. And then I do it again. Instead of choosing men that cherish me, I fuck up again and end up stranded in The Hamptons.

"Joel," I murmur.

He acknowledges me. Knows me. Supports me. Sees me. Hears me. The real me. As easy as it would be to wrap myself up in his arms, to allow him to envelope me in his warmth and love, I'm too scared to fuck it up. I've already fucked it up. Yo won't answer my calls. I'll just hurt Joel and their family even further.

"God, I'm so...so..."

I cry some more, looking around for some signs of life and a place to cool down. I pace. The concrete floor setting my bare feet on fire.

"I have to get home." Afraid I might get attacked by a deer or kidnapped by a rich Long Islander and be forced to be his concubine, I grab my cell to text the one person I shouldn't.

"Jay kicked me out of his house," I type. "It's bad. *Please* don't hate me."

Speech bubbles appear under the message and disappear seconds later. I hold my breath, waiting impatiently for any kind of response. A thumbs up. A bat symbol. *Something.*

"Send me the address," Joel replies.

My shoulders slump. I sob tears of joy, shame, and relief all at once as I share my location and thank God for men like him.

ALL IN

Yo's black Audi rolls down Jay's 10-foot driveway. I lift my chin and wave Joel over. My stomach flip flops as he parks 6 feet in front of me and the engine comes to a stop. It's been hours since I've eaten and 3 hours since Jay kicked me out of his home, but the ache in the pit of my stomach isn't a hunger pain. These butterflies are all for Joel.

"Willpower, Candi," I say to myself, despite my deep desire to throw my arms around his neck and kiss his fluffy lips. "Don't fuck this up any more than you already have."

The passenger door swings open. My mouth agape, I yell, "Yo!" and run toward her, falling into her arms. "You came! I miss you so much!"

My tears cover her bare shoulder. She holds me tight and rubs my back, whispering, "It's ok. We're okay, babe."

I wipe my snot with the front of my hand and lift my head, planting a kiss on her cheek.

"We're okay?" My voice quivers. Yo kisses my left cheek and smiles.

"Joel!" She shouts, summoning her twin from the driver's seat. Hands in his pockets, Joel strolls over to us and nods at Yo.

"I'll leave you two to talk."

Towering over me, she plants a kiss on my forehead and heads toward the car. She shuts the door behind her.

"Candi," Joel whispers. "What are you doing to me? Why did you come here?"

"I got scared...about us," I say. "What if I...what if we..."

"Don't work?" He finishes my sentence.

My eyes well up with tears again and a teardrop escapes. Joel catches it, wiping it away before it trails down my cheek.

"We've been best friends for 20 years. I *know* you, Candi Cane. I've watched you choose these assholes," Joel motions to Jay's mansion, "wondering why you didn't see me. I've been right here, right in front of you."

"Oh, Joel!" I wrap my arms around him and caress the back of his neck with my fingertips. "I didn't think I deserved you. You have a great job, family. You're going places..."

"Why do you think I date women but I've never taken any of them seriously?"

I blink, searching my mind for answers.

"Because I've always loved you, but I didn't think I deserved *you*." Joel tightens his grip on my waist. My face grows hotter. My heart pounds. I long to kiss him.

He cocks his head and kisses me lightly on the lips, as if he's read my mine. "You're talented, charming, sexy, and have the biggest heart. You're amazing."

I look deep into his eyes as they twinkle in the sun with this revelation, this unveiling of truth. He rubs my back, pulling me in closer, our groins against each other. "So, what do you say, Candi Cane? Let's give this a shot."

I look over at Yo who is sitting in her car, chair dancing to *Dakiti*. I cross my eyebrows, afraid that one day I'll have to choose love over my best friend.

"What if we sabotage this? What if I fuck up - again? You and Yo would never speak to me again."

I lay my head on his shoulder and take him all in as he continues caressing my back. Eyes closed, I mutter, "I don't want to lose either of you."

"You won't," Joel coos in my ear. "I've spoken to Yo and she now understands that this isn't just a fling for either of us. And guess what?"

"What?" I sigh, melting into the comfort, love, and familiarity that is him.

"I got you. If you get scared, talk to me like you always do. I *got* you."

I look up at Joel and smile shyly. Lifting my head from his shoulder, I bite my lip.

"What are you thinking?" he asks. God, he knows me so well.

"That I...I..." I pause, struggling to express the feelings I've suppressed all these years.

Joel pulls me closer. He cups his hands around my face and leans in. Our lips touch, our mouths part, our tongues intertwine. I giggle from pleasure and joy.

"*Oye!* Get a room!" Yo calls from the car, her head popping out of the window. She claps at our displays of affection. "Wepa! There's going to be a second wedding!"

We sway from side to side as Yo plays Karol G's "Provenza" next and pumps the volume up. I sing to Joel in between kisses, "*Baby, qué más?*"

His eyes beam as a mischievous smile spreads across his face. Joel cups my ass and lifts me off the floor. I wrap my legs around him and take him in, sucking his luscious lips as he holds me up.

"*Qué más*? That I love you, too, Candi Cane. I love you, too."

EPILOGUE

Yoanna

"Love in an elevator! Lovin' it up 'till I hit the ground!"

I poke Joel in the ribs as he begins to whistle the rest of the Aerosmith classic. Only I can't stand this song and its overly sexualized romanticism. Who wants to make love in an elevator while plummeting to their death? And who says "make love" anyway? Not me.

I, Yoanna De Santos, better known as Yo and soon to be Yoanna Rodriguez, am a realist. Joel? He's a former closeted romantic that sprung right out of the closet thanks to his relationship with my best friend, Candi.

"Ugh, you know how much I hate that song, bro!" I cover my ears with my hands and stick my tongue out at Joel.

"You just need some *real* love, sis, to know what it feels like to love when shit goes down," Joel throws his head back and laughs, slapping his lap as if he were the opening act at a comedy club.

"I do have real love," I say. "As a matter of fact," I grab my phone from my white Dolce clutch, "let me text Pedro now. He should be here soon."

And when he arrives, I'll show Joel that my relationship with Pedro is just as exciting as his relationship with Candi. We might not suck each other's lips off in public, but our relationship, ahum, *engagement,* is solid. Pedro and I have a stable, committed partnership and soon, marriage. We have our issues. And, yes, we get in relationship ruts, especially when Pedro is in a funk, which lately has felt like an ongoing episode of *Days of Our Lives*, but we're a team.

"Come on, sis! Let's party." Joel interrupts my train of thought.

The elevator doors open and I step out and into my OBGYN office, which is decked out in red and gold to celebrate Christmas Eve. I scan the crowd that has gathered for the annual event, which I now host at my practice instead of Mami's living room in Washington Heights. It feels good to invite my family, friends, and loved ones to spend Noche Buena inside of the walls of the business that I've built from the ground up at only 30 years old. Well, 31 in 2 hours.

Yup. I am a Christmas baby. A tough day to be born on since everyone is focused on traveling, last-minute gift shopping, Jesus, and who they'll kiss under the mistletoe.

It all goes down at midnight, which happens to be my time of birth. That's right. I was born on December 25th at 12am. I am nothing if not a punctual overachiever.

"Hey baby!" Candi rushes towards us, throwing her entire body on Joel's. They go at it, making out right in front of me like I don't exist. But only for a second. As Candi sucks on Joel's lower lip, she reaches for my shoulder and pulls me in, slightly detangling from my twin brother and hugging me tightly with one arm.

"My two favorite people," she gushes. "Come on! Let's take shots before the big announcement."

Candi looks up at Joel, her eyes twinkling. He winks at my best friend in agreement.

"Announcement?" I ask, puzzled. "What are you two keeping from me?"

They beam; cheeks flushed with excitement. Joel nods, giving Candi the go ahead to reach into her back pocket and slide a 3-carat halo diamond right on *that* finger.

"Are you two?" I gasp.

Joel and Candi have only been an item for 5 months. Pedro and I were engaged after 3 years of dating. Maybe this is too fast, but they look *so* happy. I'm not here to rain on their Idealism Parade - at least not today.

"Yo," Joel looks at me with narrow eyes, "don't be negative. We know how you can be with your timelines, but this is me and Candi."

He looks at my best friend and his now fiancé. "This is us." Joel plants a kiss on her forehead. She leans in and rubs her cheek on his.

"We're happy, Yo," Candi assures. "Be happy for us, okay?

I sigh, nodding my head in agreement although I still have my concerns. Joel and Candi are always jumping into things - relationships, sex, jobs. They aren't steady or methodical like Pedro and I. But I want them to be happy. God, they look *so* happy.

"You have my blessing, okay, babe?" I say to Candi, giving her a smile. "You both do."

Candi claps, giggling with excitement. "Let's go, baby. Let's tell the world!"

Joel smiles wide, his dimples deepening. I watch them walk through the crowd and onto the mini stage that will later serve as the spotlight for bad karaoke crooning, aside from Candi who can blow like Beyonce. Unlike Pedro who sounds like a dying frog. Speaking of, where is he? His shift ended 2 hours ago and he hasn't responded to my texts.

"Please don't ruin tonight with your mood," I whisper to myself, pulling out my phone to text my fiancé. I swipe up as Joel and Candi pick up the mic.

"We have something to share with all of you!" Joel begins and passes the mic to Candi.

I scroll through my text messages and see a text from Pedro.

"Joel and I are..." Candi continues where Joel left off.

I click on Pedro's text.

"We're..." Joel and Candi say simultaneously.

"I'm sorry. I'm not coming tonight. I don't want to do this anymore, Yo."

"Engaged!" Joel and Candi shout into the mic in unison.

The crowd roars, throwing "congratulations" and "we knew it!" at the gleeful couple while I stand there, numb. Because my fiancé just broke up with me 110 minutes before my 31st birthday. Because for the first time in my life I don't know what comes next.

Thank you for reading *Heights of Love: Candi*! If you enjoyed this book, I would be grateful if you could leave a review on Amazon. Reviews help boost book sales. As an indie author, they are especially helpful!

Love,
Sujeiry

Can't get enough of Candi and Joel?
Download a free bonus scene on BookFunnel:
https://bookhip.com/HMFWJJB

There's more! Sujeiry's next book in the "Heights of Love" series, *Yoanna*, is now available for pre-order: **https://amzn.to/47iFnq6**

Find out what escapades Yo gets into after being dumped on Christmas/her 31st birthday.

KEEP IN TOUCH WITH CORNER OF PRESS

Facebook page: https://www.facebook.com/
givethemromance
Instagram: https://www.instagram.com/
givethemromance
Website: https://www.givethemromance.com
TikTok: https://www.tiktok.com/
@givethemromancebooks
Amazon: https://www.amazon.com/stores/
Corner-of-Press/author/B09ZYTNM8C

ABOUT THE AUTHOR

Sujeiry Gonzalez is a Dominican American romance author, journalist, and poet, and the co-founder of Corner of Press publishing. Her spicy and often funny romance novels predominantly feature Latinx characters and capture the essence of Dominican culture in NYC. A former relationship journalist and columnist coined "The Latina Carrie Bradshaw," her articles and stories have been published in *Latina Magazine, Cosmopolitan, Hip Latina, Well + Good*, and many other publications. Sujeiry also hosted Love Sujeiry, a relationship talk radio show, on SiriusXM. Raised in the neighborhood of Washington Heights in NYC, she now resides on Long Island, NY with her son.

9 7 9 8 9 8 7 4 2 4 1 0 0